OLIVIA
the Superhero

Adapted by Cordelia Evans
Illustrated by Patrick Spaziante

Simon Spotlight
New York   London   Toronto   Sydney   New Delhi

Based on the TV series OLIVIA™ as seen on Nickelodeon™

SIMON SPOTLIGHT
An imprint of Simon & Schuster Children's Publishing Division
1230 Avenue of the Americas, New York, New York 10020
This Simon Spotlight paperback edition May 2016
OLIVIA™ Ian Falconer Ink Unlimited, Inc. and © 2016 Ian Falconer and Classic Media, LLC
SIMON SPOTLIGHT and colophon are registered trademarks of Simon & Schuster, Inc.
For information about special discounts for bulk purchases, please contact
Simon & Schuster Special Sales at 1-866-506-1949 or business@simonandschuster.com.
Manufactured in the United States of America 0416 LAK
ISBN 978-1-4814-6055-2
ISBN 978-1-4814-6056-9 (eBook)

"'*Pow! Zap! Crunch!*'" said Olivia. She and her dad were reading a *Super Force United* comic book together.

"'You'll never stop me, Super Force United!'" Dad read in a Dr. Trouble voice. Baby William shook his rattle, and Dad and Olivia laughed.

"'The superheroes jumped into action,'" Dad continued. But before they could finish the story, William started crying.

"Looks like he dropped his rattle," Olivia said. "Don't worry, William. I'll find it!"
But the rattle was nowhere to be found. *Hmmm*, thought Olivia. *I bet I could find it if I were a superhero . . .*
Olivia imagined using super strength to save William's rattle from Dr. Trouble.

"Dad, I know what happened to William's rattle," Olivia told her father. "A super-villain-bad-guy took it. And the only way to catch a super-villain-bad-guy is to become a superhero-good-guy!"
She dragged her trunk over to the table and pulled out some supplies. In a flash Olivia became Super Thinker, a super smart superhero!

If Olivia was going to catch the rattle stealer, she needed backup. First she called out her window to Francine.

"Do you want to be a superhero?" asked Olivia.

"Sure," said Francine. "I'm super fast. I could be Super Speedy Clown!"

Then Ian demonstrated his super robot hearing skills—
he could hear a fly walking across the table!

"Super Robot, you're in!" Olivia declared.

Alexandra wanted to be a superhero too. "I am Super Noisy Dancer!" she said as she did a flamenco dance and clacked her castanets.
"You sure have super loud powers, Alexandra," said Olivia. "You're in!"

"And what's your power, Harold?" Olivia asked.
"I've got a sandwich," Harold replied.
"A super *stinky* sandwich," squealed Alexandra.
"Your name can be Super Stinky Sandwich Man!"
Olivia said.

"I hereby call our superhero team The Mighty Five!" said Olivia. "Now, the first thing we need to do is find William's rattle. Super Robot, use your super ears!" Ian concentrated. "Super Robot detects rattling noise coming from in there," he said. "The evil rattle thief must be hiding inside!" said Alexandra.

"How do we get him out?" asked Francine.

"Super Stinky Sandwich Man, use your super stinky power!" said Olivia.

"Throw your sandwich in the doghouse. Then we'll grab the evil rattle thief when he tries to run away from the smell."

Harold took one last bite of his smelly sandwich and tossed it into the doghouse. The rattling noise stopped and out ran . . . Perry!

"Are you the evil rattle thief?" Olivia asked her dog. Then she noticed the box of dog biscuits he was holding.

"That was making the rattling sound!" said Alexandra.

"I guess Perry's not our thief," said Francine.

"Finding William's rattle is hard, even for superheroes," Olivia mused. "Mighty Five—we need to split up!"

So Harold and Alexandra went in one direction to find the evil rattle thief, and Ian and Francine followed Olivia in the other direction.

"Keep your ears open, Super Robot," Olivia said to Ian as they snuck around their backyard stage. "That rattle could be anywhere."

Then they stopped suddenly. There was a rattling coming from the stage!

"Mighty Five—I mean, Mighty Three, away!" said Olivia.

But when they leaped out from behind the stage to catch the evil rattle thief, they immediately collided with . . .

Alexandra and Harold!

"Super sorry, super friends," said Olivia. "We thought we heard the rattle."

"You heard my castanets," Alexandra explained. "I was practicing my super loud super powers."

"The rattle is still missing," said Harold.

"Yes, but my super thinking powers are giving me another super idea," Olivia said. "Alexandra can rattle her castanets super loud, and—"

"The thief will think it's a rattle and come looking for it!" exclaimed Francine.

"He'll walk right into our trap," said Ian.

Alexandra began playing her castanets loudly while the rest of The Mighty Five hid. Soon Francine's cat, Gwendolyn, approached the stage. But when Alexandra stopped clicking her castanets, Gwendolyn wandered away. "Keep dancing, Alexandra!" Olivia whispered loudly. Sure enough, when Alexandra started to dance again, Gwendolyn came back onstage. Olivia gasped. "Gwendolyn is the rattle thief!"

Olivia and Francine sprang out of hiding to catch Gwendolyn. Francine tried to use her super speed, but Gwendolyn was too fast! The cat bolted away into Francine's house.

The Mighty Five raced after Gwendolyn into the dining room, but there was no sight of her. Then a familiar rattling noise rang out from under the table. The Mighty Five surrounded the table and pulled out the chairs.

Olivia reached under the table and scooped up Gwendolyn, who had William's rattle in her mouth. "I guess Dr. Trouble isn't the only one who likes noisy toys."

"Sorry, Olivia," said Francine. "I never knew Gwendolyn was such a criminal mastermind."

"That's okay," said Olivia. "The day is saved, thanks to The Mighty Five!"

That night Olivia was happy to give William back his rattle. "Safe and sound, courtesy of The Mighty Five!" she said.

"Come on, Super Thinker," said Dad, chuckling. "It's your bedtime too." He led her back to her room.

"But, Dad, I can't go to bed," Olivia pleaded. "Crime never sleeps!"

"But little girls do," Dad said, tucking her in. "Sleep tight, my little superhero."